Paradise Club Members (PCM)

DEAL WITH ISLAMIC STATE'S NATIONAL
SECURITY DIRECTOR

HICHEM KAROUI

Global East-West (London)

Contents

Chapter Seven

PART TWO: Glorious Days in the Golden Age

(BOOK SEVEN)

The Morning of the Mogul

A wise report to a wise minister by a
wise citizen

(A serialised novel)

Paradise Club Members (PCM)

Deal With Islamic State's National
Security Director:
A Parrot is a Good Patriot!

Volumes in this series published by Global East-West (London)

Dedication

To the memory of Nana ...
Beloved mother...
You are always in my heart.
May you rest in eternal peace.

Note of the Publisher

THIS IS MISTER BASSAM Bourasin's admitted report as a citizen of His republic. He didn't give it a name. He initially addressed it to the Interior Ministry. Instead, it landed on my desk. I publish it as is, with no major changes to its form or content. However, because the report is around 800 pages long, it will be serialised. Here is the seventh book: *Paradise Club Members (PCM)*.

Other volumes will soon follow in the current Part Two of the series.

I also have to notice that this is a translation. The first draft was written in Arabic. The author had no intention of publishing it. In any case, it is understandably unpublishable in the country... for the same reasons that silence any samizdat.

Hichem Karoui

Note of the Author

All of the individuals in my story, as well as the country, are not made up. However, even if some characters claim to be more fictive or strange, crazier or more foolish than others, they are not required to justify their location. My country can be found throughout the Arab world. Whatever name people give it, you won't notice a difference if you pay attention.

Bassam Bourasin

"Nobody did a secret deal
Nobody was for sale
Nobody bent the rules at all
And nobody went to jail
And all of them were honest men
As white as driven snow
And lived on a higher plane
And shat on those below..."

Roger Woddis: All Clear

"And so, what could my sterile and uncouth genius beget but the tale of a dry, shrivelled, whimsical offspring, full of old fancies such as never entered another's brain — just what might be begotten in prison, where every discomfort is lodged and every dismal noise has its dwelling?"

Cervantes: Don Quixote (Prologue)

Chapter One

S EPTEMBER IST...

Six months already! The sky is overcast, and the air is wet. Since yesterday evening, the rain has not ceased pelting the roofs, walls, and cement courtyard floor. A stuttering and haggard rain in the desolate courtyard syncopates rhythmically in a weird dance. The first autumn rain brings optimism to the peasants, but it is a fantasy for us. There are puddles of water all over the dirty floor, and the gutters gurgle and growl in the dim light. The uniforms of the guards, the iron bars, the people's faces, and even the sheets on which I am writing are all grey. The clouds have infiltrated our cells and even our hearts. Everything inside my bosom is grey, like the crying sky I'm staring at.

The troops had left; they were most likely required elsewhere than prison. The civil war is no longer an urban legend. The country is divided. The Committee of Revolution controls the north and the mainland, but the south is in rebellion. The former president, nicknamed "the *Scoundrel,*" led the resistance to the new regime. They're no longer concealing the reality. On television, they have launched a campaign to push the population to support their couvolution. We now know the faces of the men who had set out to depose the president. They are a gang of seven, and their leader Abdelghani Abdelghaffar (in his early fifties) is the new President. They are all military personnel. Apart from Abdelghani Abdelghaffar

(AA), no one has a beard. The seven appeared as self-confident as gang members that had just looted the Central Bank. They bragged about their nationalism, blamed the former King, and ridiculed the couvolution of his "incompetent and renegade" ex-minister of the interior. The King was branded the 'instrument of the West', and the former president 'the renegade Scoundrel'.

On TV, the new leader, Abdelghani Abdelghaffar, looked like a short, dark man with shiny black hair, a broad forehead, and two big eyes that didn't look straight. A massive nose the size of an excellent eggplant topped a dish-like gaping mouth adorned with an enormous beard.

I was most perplexed by his gaze, as were the other detainees watching the news. We rarely see him at the palace without his black specs, which he wears even at night... We initially assumed he was blind, but it appears that he is not. Then one of the inmates took the initiative and nicknamed him 'the Phantom,' after the title of a popular comic book. Since then, we often heard in the cell that Phantom did this or phantom did that, and so on.

Meanwhile, somebody pretended to know the explanation for the mystery. The Phantom had an accident as a child. Since then, his right eye has been clumsily trying to outrun his left. The rivalry between the two eyes resulted in the most incredible phenomenon: when the Phantom looks at you, for example, beware, this is mere deceit. He is, in reality, looking at the person standing by your side. I won't deny that I've been terrified by the possibility that our President is squinting because it's commonly known that such people can see double. He can not only surprise the person unaware that he is staring at them, but he also sees two pounds where there is only one, four million where there are two, eight billion in-

stead of four, and so on. His eyes have the
power to make him rich at will. I wish I could
do the same miracle. On the other hand, this
represents a complex problem for the state's
affairs when you are in charge. Why did the
Committee of Revolution, whose members
seem to have perfect eyes, choose the Phantom
for president? This I don't understand. He is,
without a doubt, their undisputed leader. I'm
curious to know to which good star he owed
a clear view of the Palace on the fateful night
of the coup! He could have assailed the neighbouring villa while riding his tank and thinking he was attacking the presidential palace,
couldn't he? He was undoubtedly fortunate -
and the neighbours much more - for hitting his
target on the first try. But maybe he was not
driving the tank himself. As a result, it is not
surprising that the *scoundrel* escaped. AA, alias
the Phantom, should have spotted him. While
AA thought he was arresting the scoundrel,

he actually arrested another officer, most likely one of his servants or bodyguards, who happened to be by his side. The latter would be released later, but the wrong is done. That explains why, shortly after the coup, it was stated that 'the Scoundrel' was killed while fleeing. Nobody saw the corpse and nobody asked for any proof. I do not blame the Phantom for allowing his enemy to escape easily. Because he squints, he is not guilty. However, the other members of the Committee of Revolution are responsible for such a blunder, which resulted in the worst ravages currently inflicted on the country. It is clear that when they divided the jobs before the coup, they assigned AA to assail the presidential palace, although he could mistake the neighbouring villa for the target. That is a big, bad mistake that would hurt our country in many ways in the future.

September 3rd...

Today, we received a visit from one of our most prominent former inmates. It deserves to be fully recounted because it is undeniably a history page. I was busy arranging my books on the shelves, as I had done every morning since some inmates had become contaminated by the books mania when I heard a strange clamour coming from the courtyard. Curiosity compelled me to abandon the books and peer through the window.

A small group of men had gathered in front of the block that housed the warden family and the administration offices. The guards attempted to disperse the curious inmates gathered around the small group. But, as I tightened my gaze, trying in vain to recognise the faces of those men who had come to visit us, I noticed my friend Hassan in the centre. His tall stature and reddish hair made him easily identifiable. Spruce and elegant in an autumn brown suit, he was busy talking to the prison's officer-director, an unmistakable aura of authority surrounding him.

For me, it was a pleasant surprise and, more importantly, a ray of hope on the horizon. It was clear that Hassan was no longer a detainee. Nor did he look like a journalist returning to the prison where he had been formerly jailed to make a report.   The man has apparently managed to ingratiate himself with the country's new rulers and has become one of them. If he wasn't a minister, he was close to becoming one. That was easy to guess. Hassan is the Islamist mogul who has always lurked in the dark without anybody knowing his real identity. I saw the Mercedes and the chauffeur waiting for him in the yard and how humbly the prison director addressed him. The officer had just become as discreet as a shadow, all smiles and honey, bowing before the powerful man and almost yapping and yelping like a genuine son of a bitch.

They entered the block, and I lingered behind the bars of my window, bemused by the shining Mercedes and the other official cars parked behind it and wondering about the true purpose of the visit.

- What's going on out there? Do you have any idea?

My question was addressed to an inmate who happened to be with me in the library at that moment. He came in to change his book. The man was a notorious trader who I knew was Mr Aroussi's and Hassan's chamber mate before the latter's release. Half-bald in his forties, with tired features, a drooping moustache and a wide mouth beneath a pointed nose, all his physical presence was in his lazy eyes hidden behind curved brows. He seemed to be thinking and his bumped forehead got another wrinkle.

– This is the first visit of the new Director of Security, he stated flatly.

– Who are you referring to? Hassan?

– Actually, who else?

– How did you find out? I inquired, surprised.

– It's been in every newspaper since yesterday. Didn't you read anything?

I admitted that I didn't. In fact, the press had been allowed into the prison for two days, and while I didn't think it was necessary, some inmates rushed around buying papers and exchanging them. I saw no point in imitating them because I didn't expect anything other than what was broadcast on television. I was mistaken. For once, the new Director of Security appointment was announced in the newspapers rather than on television.

When the man left the library with his new book, I sat down, thinking about what I should do to catch Hassan's attention. He couldn't have forgotten about me in such a short time. After all, we were friends, even if we had some mistrust. But that was not entirely absurd in the bituminous and foggy days preceding the coup. Everyone was suspect in everyone's eyes by that point. We were all watching each other and trying to hide our terrible fear of being called political trouble-makers or just fans of the deposed king.

Hassan never told me about his ties to the military junta that overthrew the regime. He even hinted that he was opposed to Islamists. I had yet to learn how much my friend committed himself to them. Had he not made fun of the Afghan and his cohort? Indeed, he was deceiving me because he couldn't determine my true political colours. I have none, as I always say I am apolitical, but who would trust me? Hassan clearly didn't trust me.

As I brooded, I noticed the small group of visitors exiting the block and making their way to another, followed and surrounded by the guards. The warden was busy explaining something to Hassan, who listened listlessly as if bored. They went on a tour of the compounds while I stood on the threshold staring at them and resisting the urge to rush around and hail my friend. I told myself that if he went to the ward, he would visit the library, and I was right. When they finished their tour they went to the kitchens, and I prepared to greet them. A few minutes later, I noticed them walking towards the library and dashed up to welcome the Director of Security, who smiled kindly as we shook hands.

– Hello, Bassam, he said. How are you getting on with the books?

– Very well, sir. Thank you very much; it is a great honour for us. This is a wonderful day! Long live President Abdelghaffar! I exclaimed, carried away by my enthusiasm. The Revolution must continue! Long live the Security Director!

My effusive gushing had an effect. Hassan was touched and pleased by my warm greeting. He gently tapped my shoulder and said, Thank you, Bassam." And, turning to face his companions, he added, "A good guy this one, a very good guy indeed."

The men nodded and grimaced at me, unable to smile. The resentment in their cold eyes was talking. But as long as the security Big Boss was my friend, I didn't care about the others, including the warden.

– Mister Hassan, congratulations! I am truly delighted. I have always predicted a successful career for you. I was not mistaken. We have the right man in the right place for the first time.

He thanked me again and asked. Do you have anything to complain about?

I was hesitant to respond because we were not alone. My natural discretion prevented me from expressing my emotions in front of those unknown men. But he saw my predicament and turned to his companions, saying, "Please leave us alone a few minutes. We need to talk privately."

Except for the warden, the group withdrew meekly. But Hassan insisted to be left alone with me and the warden followed the others, a little embarrassed. The group stood outside the library.

Hassan gently took my arm and led me inside the room.

– Tell me, Bassam, what's the matter? Don't be afraid.

– Well, sir, I'm a little uncomfortable. I don't want to bother you with my problems.

– There is no problem at all. I can assist you, but you must empty your bag first. What's the matter?

– Well, sir, you know my story. I was jailed without a real charge. I've been waiting for my trial for about six months. I want to know if I'm guilty or not.

He looked at me, almost puzzled. He didn't seem to be expecting such a confession.

– But, Bassam, why are you so concerned? You are not guilty.

The great hope that loomed to me was becoming a reality.

– Are you sure, sir?

– I am, indeed.

– But the shrink said my charges would put me in jail for at least twenty years.

– Nonsense! He is not a magistrate.

– Then why am I still in prison, sir?

– I don't know why! Are you in prison? Really? Who said you are?

The looming great hope got clouded.

– Well, I mean... am... the hot... Ahem! I stammered.... the hotel, sir!

– Ah! There you are, maturing into wisdom. As you have stated, this is a hotel, not a prison. A fantastic hotel, the best in the capital. You must be proud of being accommodated at the expense of the State. Besides, you're well-protected and have nothing to worry about.

– But... am... sir, I am indeed proud. It's a decent hotel...

– Are you dissatisfied with the service? Here you'll find the best hotelkeepers in the country and the best cooks, waiters, and travel agents.

– Yes, sir. No doubt, but I am not a tourist.

– You are not a tourist. Who pretended you were? You're working here, aren't you?

– Yes, sir, but... Ahem... I've never been paid. Besides, if I stay here, I might lose my first job at 'Ouja bank.

– You will be compensated for each day you spend in this library. I'll see to it. However, you should not expect to be paid at the end of the month as you were previously. This is a different job and a different location.

– Well, sir, am... it's not just the money I'm concerned about. I know I'll be paid because I work in a State-supervised department...

– Exactly, well said, Bassam! This is the Department of State.

– Yes, sir. But I am not fit for the job. I was never trained to work in a library. My incompetence is...

– Bassam! Bassam! Cut the bullshit! What a lame excuse! You should be more aware of the threats to our country. This is a difficult time for everyone. Show your sense of patriotism; what the devil! I, too, had not been trained to serve as Security Director. But should I refuse the post? Is it not my duty to defend my country?

– Yes, sir, you are correct. However, am... Our country might need me more at the bank. It's my domain.

– No way, Bassam. You are wrong. I assure you that your real job is here. You are assigned to this library. Have you had any success with the inmates? Do they read more?

– Well, am... In fact, they do; I can't deny it. There has been some progress; they no longer insult me and reject books as they used to.

– Well, well, well! You can see that you are improving them. That is why I believe you will be most useful in this position. This is your true vocation, Bassam, though you were unaware of it. The bank is useless to you. In any case, it will be closed.

– Really? How come, sir?

– Because it is insolvent. Mr Aroussi, your boss, had caused a shambles. It's not only six million dollars he siphoned, but much more.

– Oh, I'm so sorry! I didn't know this. Mr Aroussi is an honest man and a trustworthy banker, though.

– I strongly advise you not to repeat this naive and unfounded assumption before anyone else, lest you be charged with complicity with a corrupt crook.

– But I am not, sir. You know it.

– I am confident that you did nothing wrong. That's why you weren't charged. I believe there will be no trial for you.

– I did nothing wrong, sir. But I want a trial. I'd like to know how long I'll stay here.

– You don't need a trial to figure it out. And, besides, why do you care?

– Because I'm concerned about my career, sir. I can't go on without knowing what I'm up to. It's just common sense.

He looked at me silently for a moment. Was He angry? As the silence grew longer, I became more circumspect. I should not have been so obstinate. Our friendship is not a reason to put such pressure on each other. I was so uneasy that I felt compelled to apologise. But then he said something completely unexpected.

– Look, Bassam, you have no reason to ask for a trial. You can think of me as a friend, but believe me when I say you're not going anywhere anytime soon.

– Why not, sir? I inquired. Didn't you say there's no charge against me?

– The charges you heard about from the shrink are faked. You are not detained because of them; any court would release you due to a lack of evidence. But that doesn't mean you're completely clean.

He paused, then added, "I am aware of your reports. I have examined some of them."

It was as if I found myself suddenly naked under a shower of iced water in the heart of December.

Chapter Two

At the time, I had no idea for whom Hassan was working undercover as a journalist. I didn't know that he was the brother-in-law of the former Director of the intelligence apparatus under both successive rulers, the King and the Scoundrel. That's why I was puzzled. And when he told me he had read some of my secret reports, I thought he did it recently, after the Islamist coup, as they gave him the post of the National Security Director.

Hassan waited to see how his last words affected me. I didn't need to look in a mirror to know that the blood flushed my face and, in a few seconds, made it livid as a sheet in the wind. I did not doubt that my reports to the previous administration had ended up in his hands. Oh my God! I never expected such a blow! Indeed, I had the impression that my reports had never reached the capital because I suspected Hamda La'war of pretending he was their author before conveying them to the secret service. I couldn't avoid him. Nor could I send my reports directly to the Ministry because Hamda was the first person in charge of security in 'Ouja, not me. Besides, he was my recruiter. I feared being rebuked or reprimanded if I did something that could overshadow him. But now, I see that my secret reports have reached the office. However, the intriguing question remained: how could Hassan know those anonymous reports were mine? I never signed any of them. Why did he assume I was the author, not Hamda for example or another resident of 'Ouja?

On the other hand, I didn't really figure out the consequences of the Islamist coup nor imagined militants storming the security services offices and getting their hands on the sacred archives with its secret files. Which they did.

As I was not harmed when the *Scoundrel* - at the time, minister of the Interior - took over after deposing the king, I continued my innocuous correspondence with the security department via Hamda La'war to the day I was arrested. But now the situation is quite different. The Islamists are the worse enemies of the former rulers of this country, and I was naive not to expect a witch-hunt. I knew I'd been burned by that point. My secret venture was doomed to failure. I ducked mutely, unable to say anything.

Hassan went on:

– You are not to ignore that what you did is worse, much worse than all the crimes of your boss. You were the king's secret agent; when he was overthrown, you shifted your allegiance to the Scoundrel. What happened to loyalty?

My protracted silence was much more expressive than any reply. In his eyes, I was as guilty as hell. But in mine, I had only followed the same guidelines upon which I founded my activity: Be always obedient to the authorities of your country, no matter who the ruler is. That's a principle I got from a verse in the Quran. For me, it is a sacred rule. After all, I served the state, not any government. Governments change. The state remains. But how would I put this to Hassan, who went from being a declared opponent of the Islamists to becoming one of their officials? He likely interpreted my silence as proof of culpability. So, he went on mercilessly.

– You cannot expect mercy from the new regime. I'm telling you the truth. You're in such a terrible situation! If they know about your little secret business, they'll behead you in a public place as they do to the enemies of the people. I feel sorry for you!

My knees began to shake like two leaves in the wind as I alternately oozed cold and hot sweat. But did I hear well? Didn't he say, "if they know"? Yes, he did. So there is still hope, a glimmer of light in the darkness. They still didn't know. I clung to the hope.

– Sir, I've been blackmailed. If I had not willingly collaborated with One-eyed Hamda, I would have lost my job and gotten into a lot of trouble. Suffice it to say, I was never paid for those reports you saw. All I had was my bank salary. Moreover, I owed my post at the bank to Hamda. So how could I have survived if I had disobeyed him? You know this country better than me. You are a journalist. Everyone needs an intermediary for any job and protection. Until recently, the Party was the *Patry,* under the king or the scoundrel president. Without the proper protection from the party, you have no home country, family, or home.

– No problem from my side, Bassam. I understand you were trapped like a novice unless you were fooling me. But the others – I mean the authorities – won't understand your reasons. To them, you are the enemy of the people! I am sorry.

– Ahem... um... Are... are you under obligation to... um... show them those reports? I am so embarrassed now.

– Ah yes, indeed you are, although it is too late. But my job is to unveil the enemies of the people and to bring them to the martial court.

– The martial court? Good God! I am no military personnel, Sir. I did not attempt a coup against the regime. I was not dealing in military secrets either, far from it.

– It doesn't matter, Bassam! I'm telling you the facts of the present situation. We have a new regime. Our country is fighting against counter-revolution, foreign spies and traitors. Martial Law is applied to all enemies of the people, among which precisely the man you have so loyally served. So you see, you are in deep shit!

He paused again, loitered picking some books from the shelves, and leafing through them, pretending to read while I was on embers. I felt all the more oppressed that I did not even get paid for those damned reports.

– However, he added without looking at me.

In silence, I waited.

– I'll consider you as a particular case. But, for now, I will keep your reports away from indiscreet eyes and keep an eye on you. I have people watching you here. If I am convinced that you are reliable to us, you're safe. If not, I don't need to tell you what will happen.

I breathed paradoxical air. Hot and cold simultaneously, which caused me a coughing fit. That was my first reaction. But it was short. Immediately, I recovered and composed.

– Thank you, sir, I said.

I was relieved as the threat of the martial court was not too close and anxious about "his" people watching me. I immediately grasped the situation. A negative report from one of those guys – maybe one I see every day in the collective cell – and I find myself on my way to face a firing squad!

– Sir, it is so kind and generous of you! But, sir, are you sure those damned reports won't fall into other ... I mean ... improper hands?

– Don't be a fool, Bassam. Do you think that I am unworthy of my word?

– Oh no, sir, no, no. I beg your pardon. I'm just a little worried.

– Well, you ought to be soothed now. I rely on you for everything that happens in this ... um...brothel! Do you get my point?

"No. Not you," I heard someone whispering to me. One of my bloody angels, indeed. I did not want to understand.

– Not very well, I'm afraid, sir.

– Don't be a jerk, Bassam. I want your attention and your talent in reporting. You're like a whore who pretends before her new fiancée that she's still a virgin! You understand me very, very well, I'm sure. You will write me a weekly report about what you hear and see in the pandemonium.

– Panda... panda...what?

– Ok. The madhouse where you live and work. I'll send a man to take the report. Did you get the picture now?

It was too clear.

– So, I'll continue to...um...

– Yes, yes, Bassam. You'll continue to spy for me. You'll not regret it. I know how to reward my loyal men.

– Sir, with due respect, you cannot ask me to do such a job.

He stared at me, puzzled:

– Why not?

– I am unfit. You did acknowledge that I've been trapped like a novice, didn't you?

I stopped before saying the whole truth. The fact that I lost faith in the state, the fatherland and the national parties, past, present and future, and I don't trust him more than I trust his government.

– Ah! But that doesn't mean that you're unfit for the job. Actually, you don't need to be Einstein to spy. Anybody can do it and succeed. It is, with the whore, the oldest job in the world. Cavemen and kings spied on each other. We continue to do the same. Besides, your reports have opened my eyes to your concealed talents, brother! You are a master in the art of duplicity. I assure you of my sincere belief that you are quite the man required for the job. All those jailbirds don't interest me as you do. But, my dear Bassam, you are as unruffled as folded. You are rather a Jack-of-all-trades, aren't you?

I didn't know whether I should feel flattered or offended. As I was still apprehensive, I said:

– You flatter me, sir. Indeed I am predilected to your cause, but... um... as a matter of fact, I'd rather forget the past. However, with the new Revolution, I realise I can be useful otherwise. So I thought of trying my hand at some... um... attempt to write down the *history of the Islamic Revolution*.

I stressed the last words to show the extent of my enthusiasm for the project. But he remained coldly unstirred. He just asked:

– Are you a historian, Bassam?

– I don't need to be a historian, sir. You've never been trained to be Director of National

Security, sir. You just discovered late that this is exactly your vocation. This is Mektub, sir. We can't change it.

– No, Bassam, I'm sorry! This has nothing to do with any Mektub. You don't believe in such inanities, do you?

– Sir, I am the son of my father and mother. They taught me that everything is Mektub. I beg your pardon, but I am a true believer. Allah is omnipotent and merciful. Therefore, we must accept our Mektub. This is what I have been brought up to believe in since childhood.

– Rubbish!

– I beg your pardon, sir, I didn't hear well.

– You heard me bloody well, Bassam. I said rubbish, rubbish! Nonsense! We should not have revolted against the Scoundrel if ever we condoned or believed in such insidious creeds. Mektub doesn't exist. You have worked for many years at a bank, damn it! Yet, even if it is in a small, barren village, nobody has heard about it. You're not going to tell me that you also believe in God.

I was shocked. Truly shocked. An Islamist who does not believe in God! That's way beyond all I could imagine!

– Of course I do, sir.

– Then you're not as smart as I thought. Listen, forget it. You're an ambitious man, aren't you?

– I am not, sir. I have no ambition whatever, sir, and I entreat you to believe that I am sincerely attached to my village, my family, and the beliefs of my ancestors, even if they are nuts. For me, living in a small town is much more important than living in this dirty capital, where the only rules are made for profligacy, salaciousness, nepotism, *arrivisme*, and money!

– The devil takes you! Are you now against money, Bassam? You have spent your life handling it. It is just unbelievable! I never saw a man who hated money, let alone if he worked at a bank! What's life without money?

– Perhaps nothing, I concede it, but people are becoming too materialistic and greedy. The new regime ought to suppress money instead of suppressing the banks; that would bring people to reason. I am willing to give the state all the funds I saved if everybody did the same.

I hoped my zeal moved him, but I only provoked his mockery.

– What a great heart! That's lavish generosity! Why not give it to the poor or charities, Bassam?

– No, sir. I don't trust them. They would dilapidate it. They just do not know how to manage money because they are not accustomed to it. I am not rich, though. I have only the savings from my salary at the bank, which is barely sufficient to meet all my needs, along with the sum the state owed me for 15 years of unrelentingly loyal service, for which I have never received a check.

– Are you kidding?

The threat in his voice was clear enough to me. Understanding that I had nothing to lose, I decided to play my joker card. I did not tell him the truth yet.

– Sir, I'd never been paid for such a danger-ous activity required by the authorities of my country.

I caught his attention. After a pause, I added:

– As a matter of fact, the state owes me an important sum of money, sir.

– Interesting! How much, Bassam?

I still remember the little audit I made of my 15-year-long service as the party's secret agent in 'Ouja. How could I forget?

– Exactly, $13.500 million, representing the undelivered fees for...um... the consultancy services.

I let him absorb what I had just revealed. His green eyes were goggling at me in disbelief. I went on:

–However, since this is a new government, I will not claim immediate payment. I desist and yield my rights to the state. I am a patriot, sir. I did what I did for the safety of my country. It is as if the $13.500 million were already transferred from my 'Ouja bank account to the Central Bank. I say this to show you I am siding with the Islamist authorities and supporting you. Me too, I want the return of the Islamic golden age. I want to see people behaving like the prophet's companions. May peace be upon him, sir.

Chapter Three

Hassan stared at me, aghast. His amazement was understandable. He did not expect such a bold claim. His silence protracted for a long moment, at which point he seemed gliding, musing, pondering and probably asking himself whether he should consider me a normal person or a fool. In contrast, his bony long fingers were rubbing his reddish beard softly.

– Bloody hell! He exclaimed suddenly. I never imagined you owning such an amount of money. You're rich!

I giggled.

– I'm not rich, Hassan.

I boldened dangerously, using his first name to address him, but he accepted my familiarity and insisted:

– No, no, no. You are rich, don't pretend you aren't now. A bank clerk who is also a creditor of the State is someone special, and the sum is not trivial.

– It is nothing compared to Mr Aroussi's multimillions, said I humbly.

– Yes, but your boss does not intend to give his millions to the State, but quite the contrary. His attempt to smuggle some abroad is a felony.

He paused, then asked: – You surprised me. I just don't understand how you were able to make all the money you claimed. Are you a private entrepreneur? Do you have some business I'm not aware of? I mean, apart from your salary, how did win $13.500 million?

– Writing reports, sir, I said simply.

– Writing reports? Are you talking seriously or wasting my time?

The tone became threatening.

– Quite seriously, sir. I made my audit for 15 years of service. I'll explain it to you. A single top-secret report costs $2500, not including storage in my archives. The price covers the following: Pens, paper, Table and chair, Electric light, drinks, Clothes and shoes – all necessary paraphernalia for writing. Multiply by 30 days (i.e., a month). You will get $75,000.00. I used the dollar because it is easier than our national currency. The cost of archiving a single report is $25. As it is a daily report, the cost is $750 every month and $9000 per year. Add $750 to $75000, and you get $75.750. Multiply by 12 (months), and you get $900.000. Sir, multiply that figure by 15 years, and you obtain $13.500 million.

– How can you prove your claims?

– You have the reports, sir. I also have the original copies, well concealed in my secret archives. With such evidence, any good lawyer would show that I worked undercover for the governments of my country. But I wasn't paid like any public servant.

– But you're the opposite of a public servant, Bassam. You worked secretly. You admitted it.

– Yes, I did. But would that suppress my right to a decent salary?

Silence. Then:

– Ok. Tell me now. You said you intended to give your money to the State. Are you still resolved?

– Yes, sir, I am. Do we have an Islamic state or not?

– Of course, we do, Bassam. I'll go further. We don't have any Islamic state. We have the real, the authentic, and the unique. Our country is now the only in the world applying the pure Shari'a, as it was known at the time of the prophet and his glorious companions. We have already devoted Muslims joining our ranks from all over the world, Europe and the USA included. Our brothers in Allah, males and females, are convinced that the Emir, Sheikh Abdelghani Abdelghaffar, is the Caliph who will bring back the splendour of Islam and rebuild the empire. We are ready to conquer the world and enforce Shari'a on the unbelievers. The Islamic empire is rising. Do not doubt it.

– Sir, I am happy to know about it. But, sir, as a high representative of the authorities, do you guarantee my safety after I promised to give back $13.500 million, earned honestly while serving the country, to benefit the Islamic state?

– I can do more, Bassam. I'll make you a PCM. As soon as you sign the official documents acknowledging your generous donation, I will issue a certificate proving that the government of The Emir of All Muslims, Sheikh Abdelghani Abdelghafar, acknowledges you as a good Muslim under the Shari'a law, which allows you to do any business you choose, marry four women or more, possess as many slaves as you wish, females and males, and travel across the country and abroad without being troubled at the checkpoints and the borders. As such, you acquire a new status. We call it in the Islamic State: PCM.

– Sir, what's the PCM?

– The pagan VIP has the pretence of being a *Very Important Personality, right?* The Islamic State does not recognise such arrogant nonsense. No individual could match or outpace the PCMs selected among the hyper-selected. The only VIP we acknowledge in this country today is the Paradise Club Member (PCM). Those persons drive their happiness from being members of the Muslim community ruled by the Shari'a law. However, because they supported our noble cause, we call them PCMs, which means they are expected in Paradise. The first in this order are the martyrs (Shahids). They sacrifice their bodies by blowing up a bomb among an unfaithful group or getting killed in the battle. The second in the ranking are people like you, Mr Bassam, who donate significantly to our cause, facilitate a crucial deal, and so on. Other services to the Islamic State may also have the same reward.

It was such a surprise for me that, for a moment, I could barely breathe. I was learning. Finally, when I managed to talk, I bubbled and gurgled like a bottle of water being suddenly emptied. I don't know what exactly I said. It should be something like: **"SSSS...Sir, I ......llllllllove theeee Is-**

sssssssslamic Staaaaate. I'mmmmmm fon-nnnnd of the IssssssslamiSssssstate. I wwwwwwanttooooo giiiiiiiiivvvve you the fffffffffunds immmmmmmmmmmme-diately."

I saw Hassan's green eyes widening dangerously. He was rubbing his red beard with a fixed gaze. If a camera was there at that time to shoot us, we would look like two crazy-mad guys trying to break out of a psychiatric block. I saw him shaking his head as if to expel some odd idea that haunted it. I don't know how long our madness has lapsed. He was the first to speak.

– But we are not asking you that much, Mister Bassam. You can keep some funds for your private projects.

I noticed with relief the 'Mister' that infiltrated his words. I could only relish with agreeable titillation the congenial change in the mood of my interlocutor.

– Sir, I want to be a PCM! I know the Islamic State does not need my money to survive. The state can get any money from the citizens using legal means. I hope you don't think I am miffing the Administration with my proposition. I am neither a malevolent renegade nor a conceited braggart. A concatenation of events made me think it would be unduly frustrating to restrain myself from showing my indefectible loyalty to the Muslim empire. That's a big change because I intended to claim my rights from the former Administration.

– Didn't you do?

– No, I didn't. I was thinking about the best way to do it. Should I hire a lawyer? Should I talk to the media? Should I ask the administration directly? What are my chances of getting heard? Should I go to Europe and campaign for my rights with the help of Human Rights Associations and the press? Should I write to the former president or to the UN secretary-general? While I was still speculating, two men came to my apartment in 'Ouja to take me to the...Ahem... "Best hotel in the capital"! So they said. As I thought I knew them, I followed them.

– So you knew them?

– No, sir. I mean, yes. I thought they were my angels disguised as civilian State police.

For the first time since we met, Hassan crackled a laugh. I didn't understand what was funny in my talk. Then, as my facial expression veered to disappointment and anger, he stopped abruptly. To hide his uneasiness, he turned to look at the shelves. But I knew that he listened to each word I uttered with attention.

– I understand your noble motives, he said. I won't fail to convey them to the Minister eventually. However, this is something that must be duly rewarded, Mister Bassam. It may even forgive your previous misdeeds, although that must be settled legally. It would be much more presentable to the high spheres if everything is clear on this level. We don't want anybody to think of some kind of bribe, do we?

– You are perfectly right, sir. I agree with you. I'm not starting my new life in the Islamic empire by bribing the officials. I'll ask Mister Ammar to take care of this issue.

– Who is Mr Ammar?

– Nobody, sir. Just my lawyer.

– Ah! Good! Tell him to prepare an agreement. Or, wait. Maybe we'll prepare the legal documents for you. By the way, you probably want something in return, don't you?

– Don't misunderstand my purpose, sir. I'd be offended.

– Sorry! I didn't mean. I only want to ensure that you will not regret your action.

I hesitated, then said:

– Well, I won't regret it, sir, if it can help forgive my ...Ahem...um ... previous misdeeds.

I mean..um... if those reports you hold at the ministry could disappear ... vanish... completely, who cares? And I will be relieved, sir.

He cleared his throat.

– Hmmm. I'll think it over, but I promise you nothing. Well, let's say it may be negotiable.

– I am glad to hear you say it, sir. I am sure we can reach an agreement. Since you are also a PCM holding those state documents, it's easier for me. Have you got any idea about the way we can settle the matter? I mean before reaching paradise while we're still on earth.

Hassan pondered, rubbed his moustache gazing at me straight in the eyes, then said:

– Yes, indeed, there is a solution. I need to reconsider the whole situation in light of what you unveiled. It will not be hard to release you, but I want to be certain about your projects in the near future. What do you intend to do when you get out?

– Oh, nothing special, sir. Nothing different from what I was doing before. I will very likely go back to my bank.

- What if you find the bank closed?

– Then, I will seek a post in another. With 15-year experience, it won't be hard to find something convenient. I'll be sorry to lose my post at 'Ouja bank, though. I got attached to my old customs. I think you know I am a grand sentimental, sir.

– Oh yes, indeed you are! It is hard to discern the truth from the false in the present circumstances. But do not misinterpret my thoughts, please. I view your goodwill gesture with consideration! Any help is welcome in our hard conditions. As you know, oil, our main source of income, is presently in the hands of our enemies. I should not tell you this, but you are now one of us. Our finances are in a pitiful state. I didn't tell you that we discovered that the rapine had preceded our arrival. The men ruling the country before us took advantage to fill up their pockets. That's the atrocious truth about our nation. Whatever their level in the State, the men in charge plundered the country, generation after generation, for centuries. That's an awful tradition that generated tragedies and pain, still at work until we took over. Suitcases full of hard cash were smuggled through the frontiers to South America, the USA, Europe, and much more to tax havens, to say nothing of the money that had never entered the State's boxes, albeit it had been duly recorded in the registries. According to all appearances, the Scoundrel and some of his men were expecting to be overthrown, like generations of previous rulers. That is why they used full prerogatives to secure a comfortable retirement abroad. They bought palaces, villas, and hotels and made many other real estate investments in Europe and America; you can count their shares in foreign companies in the billions. And despite the bragging speeches, they had no confidence in the economic and political institutions of the country they were running. If they did not expect a military Coup, they were probably obsessed with looming revolts and uprisings. But all this is nothing compared to the vicious behaviour of conveying huge funds to support or merely provoke coups, countercoups, rebellions, and political unrest in remote or neighbouring countries. You would be shocked if you knew how much they had been involved in covert operations and seditious activities abroad. In contrast, they kept saying at home,' "We want peace and friendship with all the States'! So it was that when we took over, we discovered - to our horror - that the country was drifting. The cash in the central bank was barely sufficient to cover our expenses for six months. Now, with the war in the south, you can imagine the situation; I don't tell you.

He paused, fished into his jacket's pocket for a moment, and then asked me:

– Have you got any cigarettes? I've forgotten my packet.

– Sorry, sir, I don't smoke.

– You did good, he replied. In paradise, nobody smokes.

– How about drinking, sir? I mean beer, wine, whisky…?

– Allowed, he said while raising his hand, to beckon towards the men still waiting for him outside. Did you not read your book?

– The Quran, Bassam. What the hell! It's allowed.

Almost running, one entered the library and stopped at a step from us, giggling and frisking about like a well-trained fox terrier.

Chapter Four

– Give me a cigarette, said Hassan peremptorily.

– Yes, sir.

The fox terrier rummaged in his pockets and produced a packet which he handed politely to his boss, insisting that he kept it. I noticed the cigarettes were of the same US trademark Suleiman Mughli used to smoke. The fact did not escape me, for that particular brand is rare, at least in our country. And momentarily, I lucubrated in the dark about the possible connection between Hassan's bodyguard and the Mughli. But since it was an insoluble problem, I forgot about it.

– Thank you, said Hassan after lighting his cigarette.

The fox terrier withdrew to join his companions, chatting idly not far from the library. The courtyard was nearly empty, apart from a dozen grey uniforms loafing around with their rifles on their shoulders. It was a quiet morning, with an unruffled sky and a warm sun. Habitually, the inmates should have been strolling along the walls, loitering around the basin, chatting or reading newspapers, shaving or washing their laundry. But the unexpected visit of the director of security had seemingly changed the daily routine.

– Well, what were we saying? Hassan asked.

– About the piteous state of the finances, sir.

– Ah! Yes indeed. It is a disaster. However, this is not really what troubles me.

He paused and, continuing to smoke silently, ducked as if trying to remember something. Then, lifting his head, he said: "Did you say that if you were released, you'll go back to 'Ouja?"

– Yes, sir, it's my home.

– Well, I don't want you to go back home. I need you here, in the capital, with me. I have something for you.

I was apprehensive about the capital but could not express my worry lest I made him angry.

– I am at your service, sir.

– Good! Are you married, Bassam?

He surprised me. It was not exactly the question I was ready to answer, for I was still flustered by what had happened since the damned couvolution. I was willing to believe I was happily married to the invisible Dalila, but I could not prove it either. Hassan did not believe in Mektub, which meant he would hardly admit that I was married in the unseen world, just as Haj Mukhtar was to his Jinni princess. So, I told myself that if I answered yes, he would check and find no wedding record because he naturally could not see the unseen. The marriage certificate may exist, but in the invisible realm. Thus, he will think I am a liar, destroying our inchoate entente. To prevent such a disagreeable situation, I was compelled to lie and pretend I was still a bachelor. It was a bizarroid situation wherein I had to lie to preclude the other from thinking I was a liar!

– No, sir, I am not yet married.

– Bachelor? That is very good, Bassam!

– I was actually about to marry in the...um... visibly, I mean in July. Ahem! It was just impossible to do it normally, sir.

– Why impossible?

– Are you joking, sir? In July, I was in jail!

– You were? Ah, well! Never mind, it doesn't matter. Anyway, you're no longer in jail. You can marry when you wish.

– Thank you, sir. I will.

– Anyway, it is not a catastrophe not to be able to marry in July. Take another month. I have a better idea regarding your money. You should marry and settle down in the capital. I'll help you with an interesting job. If you want to continue working at a bank, we will appoint you even at the Central Bank. You'll have a promotion, and you'll be responsible of a whole department. If you want something else, just tell me. However, I have only one condition.

Utterly thrilled by what I had just heard, I said eagerly:

– Thank you, sir. I have already accepted your condition.

He loitered a good moment, smoking and staring listlessly at the shelves while my impatience reached unprecedented heights. Then, he said:

– I know you are somehow puzzled, although you said you accepted the condition without even knowing it. You should not do that, because it is an important subject. It will bind you. (Pause) I want you to think about what I will tell you. No rush. Take time. Think it over. We're not in a hurry.

– Sir, I think that with good will, we can reach an agreement.

– Fine! Then look. Forget your lawyer, this is a bargain we can settle together without his help. Since you say you are a bachelor, I've got a good party for you.

– A good party? I repeated, not without amazement.

– Yes, I mean a lady or a bride if you prefer.

I started saying that I was in love, and before I mentioned the name of my fiancee, Hassan interrupted me briskly:

– In love? You aren't serious, Bassam, are you? Nobody falls in love nowadays. It's old-fashioned. Besides, you are not a teenager anymore, but a mature man. So you know where your interests are. As a matter of fact, the bride I am proposing to you is not a stranger but my sibling.

Flabbergasted, I repeated:

– Your sister?

– Yes, indeed. She is the woman that fits you more than anyone else. Do you trust me?

– I trust you, of course. But, um... in truth, I was not expecting your proposal. It is too much honour for me, sir.

– I knew you would be surprised. That's why I asked you not to give any answer before thinking it over quietly. Let me tell you this, Bassam: My sister Sophia is your lifebuoy. Not only can she release you with a single word, but she can also open locked doors to you.

I was so stunned by these revelations that I was barely able to stutter:

– Is she, um… so powerful?

He giggled.

– You can say that she is, yes.

– But I thought you more powerful, sir. You are the Director of the Security!

He smirked and said almost in a confidential tone:

– Between us, I am not ashamed to say that Sophia is not a stranger to my promotion. She is a good adviser, and besides, the new Minister of the Interior is… um… Ahem! Her ex.

– Her ex-husband? Do you mean she divorced?

– Bassam, what the hell! I said she might be a good bride for you, and you ask whether she divorced! Of course, she did, damn it! They divorced a long time ago.Well, ahem! I mean before the revolution. But as they have three children, they are still on good terms.

– Three children? I repeated, more struck by the prospect of marrying her than amazed by the story.

– Yes, three. Don't feel blocked just because of that. It's nothing, she can easily have three others with you if such is your wish. Now, look. No hassle! When you agree, just tell me, and we'll pay her a visit together.

– But sir, what about Dalila?

– Oh! I warn you against ever rising this subject before Sophia. She's very sensitive, and she's well capable of rejecting your proposal.

I had to react quickly before being trapped in a situation I had never expected. I felt that I had merely to protect myself against such scrambling projects that had nothing to do with what I had previously planned for my future.

– I am very honoured, sir, but I don't think your sister would accept marrying me.

– Ah, well? Why? You're a good chap, though. Besides, you are a banker or will be soon; your little fortune is also most welcome.

– That's the point, sir. Actually, that money is pure speculation. It has no solid existence.

Dumbfounded, he asked me:

– Speculation? No solid existence? What do you mean exactly?

– I mean that apart from my bank salary, I have no other income. I reckoned that the State owed me such a sum for a longstanding service, but... um... this is perhaps untrue. They can say I was acting out of patriotism, which is not something one should deny. You understand, sir, patriotism is too flattering to discard even if it would cost me two $200 million, the exact amount of the debt they owe me.

I should not have uttered the last sentence, for it had had just the opposed effect of what I was seeking. Too late! Once again, I was carried away by my unbridled tongue, saying much more than I meant. As always happen in such a situation, Hassan omitted or dismissed the first part of my reply and retained only the last detail. Then, he grabbed my arm and opened his green eyes widely.

– Two hundred million dollars? Did you say two hundred?

Dumfounded by his reaction and eager to give my services to the State more a valuable estimation, I boasted:

– Yes, sir, two hundred MILLION dollars, and who knows? Perhaps more! One does not count these things.

I saw an indescribable joy gaining the man. He would have danced like a professional ballerina because he likely believed - at least, he gave me that impression - that the two hundred million, which I do not know how they infiltrated my sentence, were already in his pocket! Meanwhile, he omitted that I was merely speculating.

– So, it's not $13.500 million only. Are you sure? He asked me with the vicious insistence of someone who had resolutely shut his eyes and ears to the truth.

– As sure as I am seeing you at this moment, sir!

– But you are a national treasure, Mr Bassam! Come on, please, allow me to kiss your luminous forehead hiding such a genius. You're my brother, my chum, not just my future brother-in-law. From this moment onward, your desires are as orders for me. Just express your wish, and I'll shake earth and heaven to satisfy you.

To my bewilderment, he kissed my forehead, and I smelt the trickling mixture of tobacco and amber exhaling from his beard. The scene would seem quite preposterous to the group of men that were certainly watching us from the courtyard. I did not dare turn my head to look at them, but I did not doubt that I had become the subject of their idle chatting. The success did not daze me, though. I knew it was still so flimsy that the spell would break at the first breeze and swoon away. And though a kind of beatitude and gratefulness for my good star invaded me, I thought it better not to challenge fate more than I did. So, while keeping my advantage, I waited impassibly for the ebbtide, expecting at any moment the hard thwack of the reverse. But it did not come.

I had many good reasons to think the worse could still happen. I have lied to the Director of National Security, and he seemed to swallow the lie like candy. Hassan excused himself and tottered away to join his men. Then I saw him speaking to them, although I could not hear. I only noticed that they were eying me with an increasing interest that confined the indiscretion. I can't tell whether those conspicuous gazes expressed admiration, amazement, respect, or something quite different. I did not care, for I could not measure all the ravages I had inadvertently caused. Still unaware that the winds had turned favourable to me, I behaved like a lascivious jailbird.

When the Director of Security came back, he smiled and said:

– We'll continue this chat in my office if you allow me such an honour.

I thought I was dreaming.

– It is too great an honour for me, sir. I can't accept it.

– What? Why? I just sent one of my men to buy you a convenient suit. You cannot continue to wear these rags.

– I am confounded, sir. You shouldn't have sent him. I appreciate it, though. It is kind of you. But I don't want to disturb you any more. Actually, I got used to wearing these... um... rags!

– Sorry, Bassam! But I think you'd be much fitter to meet the Emir with a respectable suit.

You cannot go to the palace in such a poor dress. The Emir is very punctilious on these matters. You did see him on the TV, and you should not have failed to notice the importance he accords to his look. As you know, the seven members of the Committee of Revolution are all military officers. Still, they are now dressed in civilian clothes, and you can trust me if I tell you a State secret. You are now one of us. My ex-brother-in-law, Minister of the Interior today, is a loyal customer of the greatest Parisian and Londoner tailors. Four times a year, he used to visit Paris and London with Sophia to get his clothes duly tailored, from the tie to the underpants. He has got a different assortment of garments for each quarter. And each quarter, he has a different dress for each month and each social activity. He would never wear the tie of September in August or October; it would be inelegant. Besides, you would never see him wearing the same shirt or jacket over dinner if he wore it over breakfast. Sophia would not allow such a misdemeanour. And even after they divorced, he continued visiting London and Paris four times yearly with his new wife. One never loses the good habits, and a well-supplied wardrobe is certainly the mark of a successful life. You can't deny that, can you?

Whereas he paused to light another cigarette, I was seized by the odd feeling of a man who does not know exactly whether he is living a dream or a nightmare. I was so confused that I kept silent, fearing that what I could say worsened the situation or involved me more and more in a maze. Anyway, what could I say? I was pushed before the accomplished fact. I could neither refuse what Hassan proposed nor conceal my surprise. The tide that was carrying me was too much overwhelming to withstand. And Hassan went on:

– Observe that my sister's divorce did not affect my relationship with my boss. Far from it. I still call Mamduh my brother-in-law, and he still trusts me, which is not amazing. I owe him a lot since the period that preceded the Coup of the Scoundrel. I won't hide that at the time, he used his influence as the King's Intelligence Director and adviser to get me an appointment as editor of a weekly magazine. You have certainly read '*The Friday*', before it was suspended, haven't you?

– Oh! Everybody knows *The Friday*, sir. It was my preferred magazine.

– Well, you don't know it was an antenna of the Defence Ministry, although it was not officially recognised. The military Intelligence agency was our main supporter. The real boss of the magazine was Mamduh himself, but his name never appeared in our columns.

Such revelations took me aback. I remembered then what he told me.

– Haven't you been incarcerated twice, sir? Firstly, under the King, and secondly, under the President-Scoundrel? I can't reconcile this with the fact that your magazine was...um... supervised by an official institution. I have always thought it was independent.

– Your memory is good, but you still have much to learn about politics.

He paused, puffing the smoke from his nostrils, then added:

– Nobody is independent in politics, Mr Bassam. Even the King was not independent; otherwise he would not have lasted over twenty four hours after the country's independence. Do you think the Scoundrel acted spontaneously to overthrow the King? You would be naive if you swallowed such a twaddle. The Western allies let down the former King when he grew greedy and too craving for an absolutist autocracy despite the iterated advice to rejuvenate his regime by injecting new blood into its rotten body. The old man could not grasp the extent of the changes in our society since the discovery of oil. He turned a blind eye on the claims for modernisation and democracy accordingly to the precepts of Islam as they had been thoroughly in the last years by the Islamist thinkers and preachers. When I published an article by an eminent scholar describing the insidious mismanagement undermining our economy and calling for change and democracy, I was accused of treason and republicanism and arrested along with the scholar. Indeed, Mamduh could do nothing, though secretly, he supported me. Sophia said afterwards that she could no longer live with a man who let her brother down at the worse moment, and when I explained that he supported me, she refused stubbornly to admit the evidence. The truth is that she knew about his affair. That's why they divorced. A few months after my release, the Scoundrel undertook his coup, and the bastard succeeded. My former brother-in-law was promoted to the higher echelon. As the Scoundrel trusted him, he allowed him to resume the funding of '*The Friday.*' Subsequently, I retrieved my post as editor. About three months later, the Scoundrel grew suspicious towards the magazine and ordered bluntly its suspension after a deaf and dramatic struggle between rival factions. The party wanted the magazine to be more involved with its political line, and even the Defence Ministry claimed that we were not enough keen to praise the military establishment. And to crown the whole shit, I stumbled from the seventh sky when I was summoned and informed that I was under arrest. That's how I came here for the second time, where I spent ten months waiting for a trial that never occurred when I met you. Fortunately, the revolution was creeping meanwhile.

I hesitated before asking him:

– Do you mean you were not engaged to the fundamentalists before the revolution?

He pondered.

– Well, it is a trifle complicated. But to be honest, I am engaged to my brother-in-law creeds. I am just loyal to him.

– I see, you are like me, sir... um... sorry! I mean, I am like you, indeed.

– What?

He expressed his surprise, and staring at me with suspecting green eyes, he added:

– Are you then one of Mamduh's men?

– No, sir, no, no. You're mistaken. I'd be honoured to serve him, of course. But I mean, I am like you, loyal to the persons rather than the ideas. It is much more practical.

– Ah! He sighed with relief.

There was a pause, and then he said:

– Well, you should perhaps give me the reference to your account in the treasury records.

I'll see they pay you at least a part of the debt; I can't promise more.

That was what I apprehended. I was on the brink of apoplexy. I felt I was about to crack and break into tears, but I remembered that the pig kept my reports in his grip and was just blackmailing me. It would be my end if I yielded to the pressure before obtaining the return of my reports or at least their destruction. I had been perhaps naive in playing this game, responding meekly to Hamda La'war's pressure. Still, now that I opened my eyes and saw how greedy and heinous they were all, I resolved to go about until the end of the game, if ever there is an end. Maybe I am irredeemably wicked, but they are not better. I did serve the State. What the hell! Didn't I? And I am not to be outdone easily. But who are they serving? Allah or the Devil?

– I don't remember the reference, sir, I said. You should ask the treasury. I don't think there are many Bassam Bourasin in this country. And if there are, they did not work at 'Ouja bank. So that's a good reference.

Chapter Five

Two Hundred Million Dollars! I fucking got balls!

What happened to me? I'm talking like them now? I hope my angels are not listening. Sometimes they're busy and get away with I said or done. Yup!

I knew I was gambling; most of all, it was an absurd and dangerous game. I had no reason to think that the Treasury retained my name as one of the state's fund-backers and that the sum I was whimsically claiming as a debt owed to me by the *Establishment* was by any supernatural chance recorded in its registers. That was just an absurd idea. Pure nonsense! I was either tempting fate or provoking the Devil. I bet on the disorder that was indubitably drowning the country's administration. I could always claim that the records had been wasted or stolen to spoil me of my rights. With all the funds that had vanished from the state's boxes, coup after coup, and government after government, it would not be a preposterous pretension. We had produced only generations of thieves and crooks as rulers. To follow our leaders' path in emptying the drawers of the state would not be so awful since it is widely accepted as a public good. Anyway, banished as I was, with the sword of Damocles hanging over my neck, I had little to lose. I knew my life was in jeopardy, and it would be so as long as those damned reports were in Hassan's dirty hands. They are the unrefutable evidence of my deep involvement with the rotten regimes of the King and his Scoundrel successor. My first and most urgent task is to get them back. If I succeed, I will not care for the rest.

Thoughtfully, Hassan came out of the wood like a cautious fox. He dropped his butt on the floor and smashed it with his shoe's heel :

– Well, I'll see to it. We're not in a hurry. Two hundred million dollars! This is not a sum that may evaporate easily. We'll get more weapons, win the war and kill the Scoundrel. The Emir will be happy to receive you, Mr Bassam. I've always thought you're not the guy you seem to be. Just like me. Ha Ha Ha! We're similar. Now, I understand why the Scoundrel send you to the pit. He wanted to get rid of you, didn't he? With all your money, you became too dangerous. He couldn't allow you to walk free. You could threaten his power, couldn't you? If you claimed to be paid immediately, you'd have shaken the earth under his feet, wouldn't you? And with this, you claim to be apolitical. Ha Ha Ha! That's a funny joke, man! But you are a great businessman, Mr Bassam. A luminous mind indeed, and I don't know of any apolitical businessman. Business and politics are like twins who dislike each other but are forced to cohabit under the same roof. Sophia also will be delighted to meet you. What about dinner with her this evening, in her villa? I'll phone her if you agree.

The little game was taking an unexpected turn.

– It would be a delight for me, sir, but I'm sorry because it seems impossible.

– Why impossible? Are you busy today?

– Busy? Yes, I am always busy with the inmates. I don't work after sunset, but I must be in my cell, maximum at 7 pm. If not, there will be consequences, sir.

– Are you kidding, Bassam? You speak as if you're still detained.

– Am I not?

– No, You aren't.

I hesitated. It was too beautiful to be true. I still need more guarantees.

– I beg your pardon, sir. I acknowledge I am not detained – Just a guest of this state hotel.

He became irritated.

– Oh yes, yes, but you are too modest, Mr Bassam. You're not forced to stay here any longer. I'll see to a better accommodation for you. What about the Hilton? Unless you prefer the Sheraton... Tell me what you prefer.

– Oh, no, no. It's too kind of you, sir. I just want to be a PCM.

– Please, Basssam, don't refuse. It's like in paradise, you won't pay for anything. You're still the guest of the Islamic State, with a PCM status. We don't often have the opportunity to host important businessmen. There is also Suleiman Mughli, but I dislike that man and don't trust him. He has connections with the

Mafia. His wife, an Italian lady, owns a big mall in the capital, although she spends half the year in Italy. She'd do anything to avoid paying more taxes.

– I've always wondered why a wealthy man like him was in...um... this prison with me. What did he do?

– The Scoundrel charged him with conveying guns to Mohamed Mashawir, a notorious militant nicknamed *the Afghan*.

– It was untrue, of course.

– It was true. The Mughli and the Afghan are long-standing friends, although they hate each other.

– But I was told that Mughli was behind that odious trade of East-European women, which was ordered by the Scoundrel. Why should he seek to overthrow him?

– Mughli has no principles whatever. He is not like you and me. He has no friends, no creeds, and no loyalty. The only language he can speak and understand is that of money. He who gives him more is his friend. But he would not hesitate to kill him and throw his corpse in a ditch if his interests required it. That's why he is at once despised and dreaded. You think he is a prisoner here, but he is not. In fact, nobody dares oppose him. The judges refused to attend his trial because they apprehended the retaliation of his friends in the Mafia. He will certainly get out soon. Mahmoud told me he didn't want his hands stained with his blood. I don't blame him because he's anxious about his blood.

– He doesn't seem to be so dreadfully powerful, though.

– Oh, he is, believe me.

– He once spoke to me in the library and seemed concerned with my writing.

I regretted these words as soon as I uttered them. It is awfully embarrassing this outspoken tongue I have got! It is too long, too bold, and too skittish. I don't know how to manage my life with such a loose thing rambling and rampaging in my mouth. I always say much more that I mean or not enough. Bloody tongue!

Inevitably, Hassan asked me:

– I'm curious. What were you writing?

– Oh, nothing. Just... um... Just an account of the Islamic Revolution. I told you I wish to start a book of history.

– You can't do that, Bassam.

– Why not, sir?

– Because it has just started. You cannot write the history of a movement at its very beginning. You must wait at least twenty or thirty years to do so.

– But we are living in history, sir, aren't we?

– This is not the past of the Islamic Revolution, Mr Bassam; you are mistaken, but well, it's the present time. To pretend the contrary is to confound times and to mistake the present for the past. That could be a dangerous illusion that tacks us into recessional thought and compels us to live as if we were dead. I didn't see what you wrote about the Islamic Revolution, but you can't say it is history. Anyway, I think you'd be helpful for us otherwise. Do you know why I asked you to be my spy?

– I presume you want me to continue the old job.

– Not only that. You have a unique quality Mr Bassam; indeed, it exists in other people too, but with you, I dare say it is almost exceptional. I mean that admirable gift of repeating exactly what you just heard.

– I am not a parrot, sir, I protested vehemently.

He chuckled.

– Not a parrot? Don't be offended; a parrot is not that bad. It is very useful for State security. We use parrots in our service, either real birds trained in flippant duplicity or human agents endowed with the same qualities. They are provocative agents, informers and something alike. They are altogether garrulous and gregarious, precisely the purpose of their training. A good 'parrot' can deceive and misinform those who hear him and cause any foreign agents to betray themselves. As a rule, our parrots are sociable, affable, and sympathetic even, with a traditional background. But there are other kinds of parrots, not quite easy to spot or to handle. You see, Mr Bassam, we are all somewhat parrots, each one to a certain degree, according to the extent of freedom one can afford regarding the social and politico-economical constraints. Since we live in a certain milieu, we are thus compelled to respond to its exigencies. Thus, if we think it over, we will come to the statement that a parrot is a good patriot.

– In this case, I am willing to be a parrot, I replied eagerly.

– You are certainly a good parrot-patriot, Mr Bassam, and quite useful for the state. Just tell me always what you hear, and do exactly as I tell you. You'll discover that true happiness is never saying no to the shit, but yes, yes, and step aside. Never try to remove shit, Mr Bassam, since the whole world is full of it, and life is so short; if not, you'll find yourself sinking into it up to the neck.

Such a philosophic argument could only elate me, even if it was founded uniquely on shit and aimed at its perpetuation in our life.

– I don't want to seem bragging, sir, I replied, but after a long time, I have discovered this truth you are telling me. Shit is, well, our common Mektub. I agree with you. That's why I never opposed Mr Aroussi, though I suspected some of his deals were not clean. I knew just a few times before my arrest that our bank was on the brink of bankruptcy. I was sorry, but I could not discuss these matters with my

boss or oppose him even when I noticed some
of his relatives and friends benefited from huge
loans without presenting real guarantees to the
bank. Likewise, under pressure, I yielded to
Hamda La'war, the head of the 'Ouja cell, although I knew he was not the National Hero
he claimed to be. Anyway, I had a dream that
helped me overcome all that shit if you allow
me to borrow your expression. I had always in
the back of my mind the model I wanted to
follow, the great, the magnificent, the incom-
parable John Law.

His eyelids blinked while he gently rubbed
his beard, likely puzzled by what I had just
unveiled.

– John Law? Who's that chap? Never heard
of him.

– I'm glad to inform you that he was one
of his time's greatest and ablest minds. He is
a Scot who lived between the seventeen and
eighteenth century; as he could not apply his

ideas on money and monetarism in his fatherland, he went to France, where he set up the *Banque Generale,* starting with a mere £6 million capital! In a few years, Law's bank, called the Banque Royale, became the world's first central bank. Merged with *India Company*, its shares reached the incredible level of £20.000 with a declared dividend of 40 per cent. In France, Law was adulated as nobody has been. Even the Duchesse d'Orleans kissed his hand, they said. He was a national hero - a true. He had achieved the economic miracle that nobody expected. That's why I admire him and think it is still possible to start such a project with just a small capital and then increase it gradually. I prefer to apply John Law's principles of monetarism in my own country. One doesn't need to leave one's country to succeed in France or elsewhere, right?

Hassan appeared quite interested in my revelations. He did not stop rubbing his beard and staring at me with the air of someone wondering with amazement, 'what's this chap going to say next?' He pondered for a while, then said:

– I'm really discovering you, Mr Bassam, and I'm glad to hear about your project. I share your admiration for that, um...

– John Law, sir.

– Yes, Law. And I think I can help you give this project shape and substance. I am entitled to do that. The government will welcome such projects.

– Are you serious?

– I've never been more serious in my life. You are a real treasure; we just need men like you.

– But, sir, what about the Islamic precepts of banking?

I thought it was the most thorny question that we would have to answer, but he eluded it with a motion of his hand, saying not without some irritation:

– Pffff! Don't mind that, man. We're living in a complicated world, and sometimes we'll need to speak its language, won't we?

I could not reply, for the man he had sent to buy the clothes entered the room and coughed politely to signal his presence. He was carrying big bundles and packages and seemed sweating. Hassan addressed him in the same peremptory tone:

– Ah! Mr Mongi, you're welcome; please enter and show us what you have brought. Then, turning to me, he added: These are the clothes, would you please try them, Mr Bassam?

– I am most grateful, sir. It is too kind, really!

– We'll let you alone. If you allow me, I'll wait for you in the car. I must also ring the office and call my sister. I'll come back in twenty minutes. Is it enough?

– Quite, sir. Thank you very much.

Then, changing my mind, I said: "Oh, sorry, I don't want to be a burden for you, sir."

– You aren't a burden; please don't say that, Bassam. Do you need more time to change?

– I didn't dare to ask for it, sir.

– You had to, though. How much? An hour? Two hours? More? We aren't in a hurry, you know.

Mongi had unburdened himself and joined the group waiting in the courtyard. The grey uniforms were still parading along the walls, with their guns shining in the daylight.

– I want to ask you about those bloody reports, sir. Are you sure they won't fall into inconvenient hands?

– You shouldn't worry. I promised you, don't you trust me?

– I do, sir, but I'll be much more relieved if I get them back unless you destroy them. One never knows what may happen.

– Nothing can happen, Bassam. The battles are far away, in the south. The rebels you fear have no means to reach us, we are secure in the capital. And please, don't forget I am the Director of National Security. I know exactly what is going on in the country. This morning, before I arrived here, I had just received a telegram from our agents in the south, saying that the forces of the Scoundrel had been beaten and pushed back while they were trying to break through the northern highway. Indeed, there is a blockade on the shipping of oil; the pipelines are no longer pumping, and if we succeed in protracting the blockade, they will be unable to continue the rebellion. In fact, they are hopelessly encircled. Either they give up or die in the desert. We would bomb their camps if we had enough petrol for the aircraft.

– Why don't you import petrol?

– You're kidding, Bassam! An oil exporter cannot turn importer in twenty-four hours. It's not as easy as you imagine. Besides, as we are at war, the other exporters are not eager to deal with us. I won't hide that they are pretty glad to eye our misfortune. The fewer there are rivals on the market, the best are the deals. Prices rise as demand increase, you know.

– But there are certainly enormous quantities stored in the country.

– All are in the south. It is a heartbreaking strategic mistake of our predecessors! Apparently, they didn't expect a civil war. They took no precautions with the oil they stored in a single area — our unique shore. Geography doomed the country, alas! Besides, the aircraft is in a piteous state. Many aviators fled to the south with aeroplanes; the rest were not in their best state.

Chapter Six

He wanted to allay me, but instead, he depicted a disheartening picture of the situation. I am no longer sure the new regime was as strong as it appeared. How could they win the war without oil, money, or aircraft? As a matter of fact, what we call the south swallows up half the country; the other half is less desertic but more divested. Without the blessed desert, we are nothing, just a country of the third world with a rudimentary infrastructure and nothing to bestow or display but the utmost despondency of our landscape. Mountains, hills, and wastelands compound the other half - the doomed one - where my home town, 'Ouja, is situated. And further to the north, the beguiling capital of which Hassan is so proud. From 'Ouja to the Capital, the traveller would cross miles and miles of barren lands invaded by stones, weeds, wild vegetation, excrescent hillocks, and stiffed cliffs. There is little agriculture but concentrated on the shores of the great river, which is not actually as 'great' as we like to think. How could anyone endowed with commonsense hope win the war in such conditions? Besides, I was not really afraid of the Scoundrel but of the fundamentalists, the new masters of the northern country. They would not forgive my mobilisation at the service of the previous administrations, even if it was a forced service extorted under threats, blackmails and pressure. Nobody would believe that I had been the vic-

tim of Hamda La'war and his sordid machina-
tions. I had to save my head, so I had to tune
in and cope with Hassan. I wanted to stress
that I was not frightened by the Scoundrel as
he supposed but did not dare. After all, it was
perhaps his fear that he projected upon me. I
just said:

– It is not exactly what we may call a bright
situation, is it?

– No, but don't be pessimistic, Mr Bassam.
It's not as hopeless as you think; we are still
the masters. We control the capital, the north
and the main country. We are preparing the
great offensive against the Scoundrel. When
we are ready, we will march on the south and
turn the sand and the stones of the desert into
a carpet of fire under his troops' feet. We'll
crush the hideous beast in its hideout. Tell me,
what are handful tribes of bare-foot, ragged,
half-starved beduin to weigh against our dis-
ciplined, well-trained army of volunteer mil-

itants and former Afghanistan warriors? The Scoundrel is as stupid as conceited. He understands nothing about strategy and military tactics. But look at our Emir, Sheikh Abdelghani Abdelghaffar. This is a real military strategist, a man trained by US experts. They called him the "Engineer" back in Afghanistan. Do you know why?

Without waiting for my answer, he went on: – Because he engineered the trapping and bombing of significant targets under the nose of the Russians. He never failed to kill as much as possible. He's told to be a veritable genius in warfare beside his outstanding political clear -sightedness... Ahem! He will swallow up the Scoundrel on breakfast and digest him before dinner. This is now but a matter of time, do not worry!

He is perhaps a military genius, but for his clear-sightedness, I doubted it. It is a euphemism, indeed. Believing that a squint-eyed man could be clear-sighted is self-deceptive. A joke? Certainly, and preposterous! I even wonder how and when he had been incorporated as an army officer with such a conspicuous disability. My cellmate, Dahdah, was more accurate than Hassan. He told me the Emir was a militia man. He has never been a member of the armed forces. For my part, I don't imagine him particularly skilled at the exercises of shooting. Unless he had always trained himself to aim three feet beside his target to attain it, I do not know how he could get through otherwise! This does not explain why he let his worse enemy slip easily off his hands while standing two steps away. Such a military and political leader is not very trustful; it can't be helped, but I do not feel particularly tranquil at his sight.

I am not prejudiced against him, but he does not inspire confidence. I compassionately understand his physical disadvantage. I heard of one-eyed great Generals who won wars and led their armies to victory. One may see very clearly with a single eye, but with two squinted eyes, matters are likely as different as flustered. How is General *Ab.Ab.* going to read a map? Accurately? Hmmm! I doubt it! The Scoundrel is perhaps not a military genius. Still, he has an evident advantage over his enemy: his eyes are not squinting. In the darkness of the cold nights of the desert, I imagine him scrutinising the stars and the Milkyway, like a wild cat and lucubrating on a map in his tent under a candle's flame. At the same time, his troops exult in dreams, lying in their sleeping bags like lizards beneath the rocks. And in the spilt brightness of the morning, he would expound his plan for the next operation to his officers over smoking cups of coffee. Meanwhile, the troops would smear their guns and brush their boots, waiting patiently for the great hour.

I have nothing to do with the Scoundrel since he is no longer our beloved and mighty president, cheered and feared by everybody. He is now a mere rebel, challenging the authorities, a meretricious outlaw, a brash herald of the catastrophe. But this does not mean, either, that I would put my fate eagerly into the hands of a man incapable of discerning me from my shadow. Really, I was being jammed, and in that beguiling confusion, I could neither step forward and engage sincerely in the Islamist cause nor step backwards and claim that I was still loyal to my Scoundrel-President. It is a painful situation for which I have not been prepared. And Hassan seemed not to notice it; on the contrary, he let me understand that he considers me as 'one of them'.

One of them? Me? One of whom?

They are sheltered in sumptuous villas and luxurious palaces, driving expensive motor-cars, holding astronomic accounts in foreign banks, gambling millions and millions in the casinos from Monte Carlo to Las Vegas, losing them happily as if they lost old socks, betting millions on the stock exchange's shares, manipulating thousands of men and leading them to the death-trap as if they were a cattle of calves, not giving a damn for their lives and that of their wives and children; while their own families are skiing airily on the snowy mountains of Switzerland, or sunbathing on the golden shores of the Riviera, unaware of the despondent plight of their people and the dismaying devastation of their country. And whether they are Islamists or secularists, royalists or republicans, nationalists or internationalists, mindful of their roots or 'don't carists', what have I to do with them? I am a simple citizen of the doomed country, a simple bank clerk, a humble labourer living on a salary. Though I am sometimes uncanny, I am not blind, though: I know very well that I AM NOT ONE OF THEM!

I may dream of founding a bank and speaking of it as if it were already true. I may talk about my projects from dawn up to sunset and between sunset and sunrise. But all this remains outside my reach. A babble is nothing more than a babble; I do not trust Hassan. As I was lying to him, it is not unlikely that he lied to me too. I never owned two hundred million dollars, not even two hundred thousand. This dream overwhelmed me so much that I became convinced of its imminence. I incubated it day and night and treasured it as a blessed omen. But it is not of idle money that I dreamed, certainly not of easy money acquired and accumulated by chance, gambling or mere speculations. I have never been attracted by that kind of roulette; anyway, I have no means to play it, even if it is only to tempt the chance.

It is of hard effort that I dreamed, not of restful rent.

After all, I am as doomed as my country and predestined to live poor among the rich! But I know that to make money, one must deal with it; this is just a primordial principle that is not hard to understand. And to make a lot of money, one has to deal in huge sums. This is different from what I was doing at the bank, for I am neither a banker nor a stockbroker, let alone a businessman. I am rather a scribe. A clerk. And I was just scribbling, scribbling, scribbling... Eh! And when I was tired of serious work, I played with Samir's innocuous games. I asked him foolish questions to know to what extent he was really clever. And he was certainly competent and as proficient as ten, twenty, or fifty scholars. And I was super excited by his broad knowledge, and I wanted this to complete my scant education. So he helped me along with Mr Aroussi, who was the first to inform me thoroughly about John Law. That's how I connected with one of the brightest minds in the banking business. I was - I am still - so infatuated and ravished by his career that I found myself repeating his name in my dreams and perhaps even in my nightmares, along with the terms of the persons I cherished, Dalila, my mother, Zerga, Samir, and Mr Aroussi.

This is the real world within which I found myself confined to live. It is as solid and strong as the rocks of our mountains or the rusty bars of my cell. Nothing could shake it, snatch it from me, not even the most storming hurricanes, and certainly not a Scoundrel, even if he was a former president, let alone a group of lunatics. This is at least what I believed until the sudden entry of the black guard, Mahmoud, bringing the darkest news I had ever heard.

He stormed into the room with a telegram in his hand and said:

– Excuse me, sir, I have something for the prisoner... um... I mean Mr Bassam.

Hassan gazed at the intruder sideways and asked him:

– What's the matter? Why are you disturbing us?

– It's a telegram, sir, and it's... um... very serious.

– Come on, give it to me.

Mahmoud approached gingerly, and I noticed that he had lost a button on his shirt so that his protruding belly obscenely showed off its swarthy complexion through the breach. It was rather disgusting, and he did not seem aware of the mini strip tease he was displaying. He handed the telegram to Hassan and stepped aside, staring at me gloomily. I never thought him capable of sadness, albeit I did not understand the full significance of his gaze before knowing the message he brought.

I stared at Hassan, who became quite disturbed as soon as he read the telegram. Then, addressing me, he said:

– I didn't want you to know it earlier, he grumbled suddenly. But I think it is now useless to conceal it any more. Be courageous, Bassam. This is God's will. I present you my sincere condolences.

Dumbfounded, I remained silent. There was a heavy uneasiness between us while my heart thumped like mad. Then, he broke the silence again and said bluntly:

– I feared to shock you if I broke the news as soon as I heard it. I wanted first to prepare you for the future. These are crucial moments in our life Bassam; be sure of my compassionate sympathy.

It was at that moment that I dared contemplate the unthinkable. I said with a stuttering voice:

– What... what happened, sir?

Again that empty look in Mahmoud's eyes and the devastating words flowing through Hassan's lips:

– Your mother and your fiancée. Both... have been called to the heavens. Be courageous, old boy.

– Called to heavens? You don't mean that they are both dead, do you?

He sighed deeply and handed me the telegram.

– I am sorry!

I took the little piece of paper with shaking hands and read it with a pang in my bosom.

Your mother and Dalila slain with three hundred residents – 'Ouja mourning – 10 hours Collective slaughter – Terrorists plundered households and shops – Town sacked –Allah is Greatest – Father-in-law – Si Houssine.

I felt the earth shaking under my feet. My head went dizzy, and I staggered like a drunken. Then, finally, someone pushed a chair behind me, a hand touched my shoulder, and I was seated, wincing and tipsy. I don't remember how long I remained mutely impounded into an encompassing sulky maze, struck by the acatalepsy of the news. Voiceless and sad, I could not imagine the hateful cabal that occurred, with its sad procession of reckless vengeance, its odious libation of blood, and its morbid display of gratuitous violence. It was too inhuman, too horrendous to be true. Why should any party undertake such an atrocious massacre? What's the meaning of slaying mercilessly three hundred people in a village of about one thousand inhabitants? Who profits from such depravity of murderous violence?

Then I broke into tears. I wept bitterly, unrestrainedly, almost with a titillation of pleasure—the pleasure of someone pouring his soul through his tears because of his impotence. And I felt that I was forsaken and alone like a derelict and worthless stone. Desperately, I had hitherto clung to a faint hope that loomed in the desert of my life like a glittering rainbow after the dreary storm. I knew I had been unjustly imprisoned and disgraced. However, as long as the little world I had been forced to leave was still palpably strong and well-shielded, I nourished the placating dream to get out and retrieve it. But now, it is over, forever. I have nowhere to go, nobody to see. I am like a straw carried away by the scuttling wind. I am nobody.

Someone was speaking near me. I heard my name. He was speaking to me. The voice was coming over from a remote place with an echo:

– Mister Bassam...sam...sam... sam...

I lifted my head. Through my tired eyes, I stared at the face of the man, trying to ease me. I could hardly recognise him. It was Hassan, though, as if a whole century had passed since we spoke. He handed me a handkerchief.

– Thank you, sir.

I wiped my tears. I never wanted to weep like a child before him. The black guard had left the room; we were alone again.

– I'm sorry! I was going to tell you, but ...

– So, you knew...

Silence.

– Since three days.

– Why, sir? Why did you let this happen? It's my hometown, my family, my flesh and blood.

Silence. He lit another cigarette with nervous movements. His hands were a trifle shaking. He was looking at the courtyard. I followed his gaze. The prison enclosure was a large square surrounded by high walls and barbed wire. The ground was covered with gravel and dirt and a few patches of grass and weeds. The men in the yard were scattered in small groups, talking casually or smoking cigarettes. Some of them glanced at the library, but most ignored us. They looked bored and resigned as if they had accepted their fate and had nothing to hope for. They laughed at some jokes or stories, but their laughter sounded hollow and forced. They did not care about me or what would happen to me. Maybe they knew that I was doomed, or perhaps they were too numb to feel anything. The sky above was clear and blue, with a few white clouds drifting by. The sun shone brightly, casting sharp shadows on the ground. It was a beautiful day, but it felt like a mockery to me. How could the world be so calm and peaceful when there was so much injustice and violence? How could the order of things remain unchanged when so many lives were destroyed? How could I face the executioner when I had done nothing wrong? The group escorted the Director of Security was still chatting perfunctorily. I overheard laughter. They were quite indifferent to my fate. Did they know too? The sky was serene, with only a few white clouds scuttling towards the north. It was a sunny day. Nothing could spoil that peaceful quietness or change the order of things, not even the massacre of 'Ouja.

Notwithstanding death, havoc, and disasters, the world will continue to live on the same rhythm. What three hundred people slain in a small anonymous village of the third doomed world will weigh in the balance? After all, it is a civil war, and nobody ignores it.

– I didn't know or even suppose your mother and fiancée were victims. You have the right to know, but as you can see, it shocked us as much as it scared you. It is so horrific that the government decided to inform the citizens after knowing more about what happened. It is a delicate matter, you know. People would think the government does not protect them, and we fear a general panic. That's why we kept silent, waiting for the adequate moment.

– But they will know, sir, they will know. You can't hide the massacre of hundreds of people eternally. This is not a small and trivial homicide but a holocaust. You are the rulers and responsible; if you conceal the genocide, you'll be accounted for it. What happened to the police and the National Guard? Where was the army you are so proud of? Why did they allow such a slaughter to happen? Who are the criminals? What is the good of maintaining a government if it reveals itself to be so impotent? The people would ask, sir.

– I know that Bassam, but I suppose you understand our reasons. But, of course, we must first catch the criminals or at least some of them, and they must confess their crimes publicly. I also assume you guessed who they are; the evidence against the Scoundrel and his men is quite clear, isn't it?

– No, sir, it is not evident as you suggest. I am sorry. You are the Director of Security, you are better placed to know, and I don't think your job consists just of suppositions but in showing strong, consistent evidence.

Chapter Seven

Boldened by my anger and despair, I could not control the furious stream thrusting from my pain. I didn't realise I was indirectly charging the new regime with genocide. As Hassan did not reply, I went on:

– ' Ouja is in the region your government holds under control. Unless the police and the army turned a blind eye to the SOS appeals, I don't know how all that could happen. Moreover, the men of the Scoundrel are far in the south; you told me just before the arrival of the telegram that they had been beaten and pushed back by your troops while they were trying to thrust forward towards the north. How did they arrive at 'Ouja - despite the blockade? They needed to cross the desert, undetected by your men, and travel hundreds of miles across hills and mountains before reaching my village. Once there, they would shoot, kill, and rampage for hours, then flee to their desert, unnoticed and unpunished. Would you explain that to me? I know 'Ouja. There is only one main street in the town, where the police and the National Guard have their stations, the bank, the post office, and other administrative and commercial offices. It should not be hard for the police to notice the criminals' arrival, stop them, or call for support. They could not possibly have been deaf and blind, whereas the slaughter was going on. 300 people! How did they manage to kill them without alerting the government law enforcers?

– I understand your anger and resentment, but I plead with you to believe I am sincerely moved. We could do absolutely nothing. When we heard of the massacre, it was too late. The first thing the men of the Scoundrel did was cut off the village from the country. Telegraph and telephone poles were completely off-use when we arrived. The police and the National Guard had been slaughtered along with the inhabitants. I had never seen such a disaster in my life. I could not believe it. Older men, pregnant women, girls, and even children and babies had been atrociously slain, and their corpses bear the indelible marks of heinous torments and torture. It was not the misdeeds of human beings but wild beasts. I could not eat anything for at least twenty-four hours after I saw the hideous massacre. I am the first to mourn for the victims, Bassam. Nevertheless, I won't hide it; we cannot control all parts of the national territory. The country is vast, and we

are still organising ourselves, and we need men,
guns, and military equipment. That's why the
Emir ordered us not to disclose the tragedy before knowing more. We have been after them
for three days; if we can only catch one or
two, they will confess their crimes before the
TV cameras, and the world will learn what the
Scoundrel did.

I was blurred and abashed. Why should I
believe Hassan? Were the Islamists incapable
of perpetrating and throwing the odious crime
upon their enemies? What would stop them
if they decided it was a good tactic to smear
the rival? But if they were the true responsible,
why should they preclude the widespread of
the news? It would be much more useful to
them to point their fingers at their enemies and
say: Look what they did! It would be a sensa-
tional advertisement for them. Yet, they kept
silent about the crime, as if they were ashamed
and apprehending that their accusation back-

fired or perhaps because they were not entirely clean.

The question was burning my lips:

– Why, in your opinion, did the Scoundrel order such a heinous genocide? How would he profit from the death of hundreds of innocents? Had he become stupid after being removed from power? Doesn't he know that this is a war crime which would not remain unpunished?

– That's why we call him the Scoundrel, replied Hassan flatly. He is capable of much more horrors. He is an evil mind.

– This is not an answer, sir, I grumbled. You are a top-level official...

He interrupted me angrily:

– You don't stop reminding me of my responsibility. I am not the sun. I don't shine over the whole damned world! I am responsible, yes, but I can't be everywhere simultaneously. Come back to your senses, lad. I know your mother and your fiancée had been killed. I am sorry for that. This is no reason to charge my government or me for such crimes. I have already explained to you how the whole thing happened. Do you want me to recognise that our power is still flimsy, faltering, and weak? I did that, too, didn't I? Do you want me to shout on the roofs that we hold nothing but the capital and some villages and that the largest part of the country remains out of reach? Do you want me to confess our failure publicly to comfort you? Look, Mr Bassam. I have been very patient and kind, but my patience is not illimited. Don't forget that the reports you wrote to our enemies incriminate you in the eyes of our people and make you one of its worst foes. Don't ever forget that if you are still among the living, it is well because I've been tolerant. But you are not yet safe. It would be best if you first thought of saving your head. In the country's present conditions, with all the evidence accumulated against you, a military court would sentence you to death. We have already executed dozens and dozens of traitors and corrupted people. I offered you a good compromise, a very honourable issue. And instead of thanking me, you almost charge me for killing your mother. It is unfair!

He paused, took a long inhalation from his cigarette, puffed the blue smoke through his mouth and nostrils, and ducked as if he were regretting his unrestrained anger compunctiously, but discovering that it was too late, he stepped towards me, put his hand gently on my shoulder, and said:

– I am sorry, Mr Bassam. But, please, don't grudge. I sincerely apologise to you. I know you are deeply moved. If it happened to my family, I would react the same way. I implore you to accept my condolences for your loss.

As I did not reply, he went on:

– As a matter of fact, we are almost in the same situation. If that may comfort you, I had never known my mother, for she was dead at the same moment I was born. All my life, I carried the indelible mark of guilt. And though my father remarried just a few times after her death, I have never felt innocent. Whenever I was naughty and disobedient with my step-mother, my father reminded me I had killed my mother. I hated him for that. As a result, I grew up aloof and somewhat withdrawn. I had a lot of difficulties when I tried to socialise with my schoolmates and little neighbours. I was quarrelsome and shy. I provoked fights. I had the impression of being unjustly aggressed continually, and I had to defend myself. My mother's death had extended its sad shadow over my life since I began to understand what was happening around me. My only consola-tion was my sister Sophia, and though she is a few years older than me, she gave me some of the tenderness I crave. I loved her as if she were my mother. That's why I am so caring for her. And some years later, when we lost our father, I was barely sorry for it. Indeed, I was no longer an infant; my sister was already married, but the sufferance I had endured as a little boy extemporised unexpectedly in a feeling of deliverance. As incongruent as it may seem, my father's death absolved me from that excruciating guilt and gave me the feeling - perhaps a delusional one - to be subsequently free. I was alone, which was not new since I had always felt alone.

There was a pause. He threw the butt of his cigarette on the floor and crushed it with his heel.

– Sophia and Mamduh asked me kindly to go and live with them when our father died a few months after their wedding. I rejected their offer, but they insisted. I was twenty years old; it was my first year at the university, and my sister did not want me to live with our stepmother, who was still a young woman and would perhaps seek to remarry.

There was another short pause.

– I don't know why I am telling you this old story; perhaps just because I feel your sorrow deeply and want to join you if that can help comfort you, or maybe because I seek to unburden myself... I never married, you know, likely because I never felt secure enough or perhaps also I don't want to have children or to bear the responsibility of another death. This doesn't seem right, but it cannot be helped. I was far from imagining my life and career in those remote years. I was turbulent and dissipated, as you can imagine a twenty-year young man who had never known his mother and had just lost his father. So, I refused to live with my sister and her husband and remained in the same house. My stepmother was about thirty years old, quite pretty, with brown hair

curling on her shoulders, two black eyes glittering with an incandescent inner flame, although
their glow had almost gone when my father
died, a small nose and a fleshy mouth. Indeed,
I used to call her Mom, though she's ten years
older than me, and our relationship had never
been easy. There was always a sort of ambiguity
hovering over it, particularly in my teen years,
when I felt the most guilty about my mother's
sudden death. And I believe that Sophia has
never admitted that another woman could re-
place her mother. I could not leave my father's
house just for a female vagary. So, I stayed. I
am still living in the same place. She had not
remarried, and she is now and since my father's death, and well before, of course, the
true mother who cares for me as if I were her
offspring.

With difficulty, I retrieved my voice and said:

– I have not got your luck, Mr Hassan.
I have nowhere to go and nobody to speak

to. I am left alone, without family or relatives, whatever. My mother was nearly deaf and cut off from the world. She could harm nobody. I just don't understand why they killed her. And Dalila was as innocent as a lamb; she had nothing to do with politics; she had no opinion and did not care whether the government was Islamist. And she was not alone in this case; most 'Ouja people are quite indifferent to the political struggle. So killing them was an absurd act that served no cause. They may be the most stupid people on earth, but this is not a reason to slaughter them. I am still appalled. I don't understand how that happened.

– There is nothing to understand, Mr Bassam. I don't think our people are ignorant because they support any ruler or tyranny. Our people are charitable but, sadly, powerless. But, the civil war is nonsensical since those who benefit from it are selfish. They are pushing us to our breaking point. The Scoundrel in-

tends to instil dread and horror in the popu-
lace to scare them away from supporting the
new authority. He is aware that our people
desire an Islamic administration. As a result,
the message is clear: the Scoundrel will punish
our people for supporting the Islamic cause.
But we will not let it happen; we will fight
back. Allah is on our side. He won the battle
of 'Ouja but not the war. We are determined
to squash him like a vile beetle. I believe you
have finally decided to support us. You're out
for vengeance, aren't you?

I was sceptical that our people preferred the
Islamists over their opponents. Nobody polled
the audience, but I said, "I don't want to take
it this way, sir."

– It's the only option you have. Of course,
it would be best to exact revenge on your kin.
How will you ever find happiness if you don't?
But, Mister Bassam, vengeance must appeal to
your conscience as much as your masculinity.

Are you a woman? Don't you have a heart in your bosom? Therefore, we provide you with the means to exact revenge on your mother and fiancée.

That was a difficult choice.

– Sir, I have always lived in peace. I'm not looking for retaliation.

– You must, he said, almost angrily. It's your responsibility.

I stumbled: – Do you think so? Really?

– Without a doubt. In your shoes, I would not hesitate. I would instantly join the militants who are now fighting the Scoundrel.

My perplexity reached an all-time high for a very simple reason. It is not my type of dude. I prefer to pass the time and forget the past. I don't see myself going through the streets brandishing a gun. If I cannot accomplish justice on earth, I prefer to postpone it until the final judgement. Except for the Judges, I don't generally deal with revenge. Then Hassan continued:

– Eye for eye, tooth for a tooth. It is the proper course of action in any typical endeavour. You will never be a man if you do not get revenge for your dead. How would you gaze in the mirror without feeling embarrassed? Mister Bassam, blood calls to blood. Life is all about retribution. What is our rule if not a kind of retaliation against the King and the Scoundrel? What is our conflict but a reenactment of the same vengeance? Look at our city; what is it if not a retaliation for our predecessors' dreary lives? When the Brits colonised us, it was a form of revenge for our prior success in the Holy Jihad. We had evicted them and the other Crusaders from Jerusalem, hadn't we? And when we battled them again to free the land from their oppression, it was another act of vengeance. So, life is a series of retributions and counter-retributions. Looking at it this way, accepting your fate and fighting becomes much easier.

"I don't want to fight," I told myself.

– You don't think I will shoot the Scoundrel, do you? You are aware that I am incapable of handling a firearm. I'm not cut out for this killer business, and I'm not playing a part in a movie, Sir. I am just a dude like you or anyone else. Look at me; do you think I'm an image? But, Sir, I have sentiments. I'm completely moved. I would sacrifice my life for my family, but they are no longer with us. It's over, completed, and done for good. I will not resurrect them even if I slaughter the Scoundrel's army.

Perplexed by my outburst, he looked at me and said:

– I'm not asking for all of that, guy. What happened to you? Revenge does not always involve physically murdering someone; there are several types of killing and vengeance. You have the option. Look at what I'm providing you for that reason; if you accept to do what I say, you'll be one of the most powerful people in this nation. I've got a plan for you that you'll love. But first, get rid of these rags you're wearing; we must get to work.

He took a breath. I suspected him of thinking to himself, 'I've never seen a more foolish person!' This is a true coward!'

– Look at me, Bassam, he said. You saw me in this hole before the revolution. You know how miserable I was. I revealed some confidential secrets to you. You know I was never an Islamist, but I am now one. Why? It's not complicated: life is in constant flux, and one must know how the wind blows to stay safe. Now, the wind blowing over our country came from the seventh century. Do you want me to stand up to it and be carried away? I'll explain further. Do you think our Minister of the Interior - my ex-brother-in-law - is a devout Muslim, praying five times a day, fasting religiously during Ramadan, and refraining from wine, spirits, and pork? Eh! Like most of our country's compassionate citizens, you most likely believe this. Therefore, even though it seems surprising, let me tell you the truth: Mamduh, my dear buddy, didn't know whether it was morning or evening when they woke him up and told him the coup had succeeded, for he had spent the entire night drinking whisky at a private club in the capital. Do you believe he was unaware that the army was planning a coup that night? Yet, you'd be mistaken if you thought that. Mamduh was the Head of Military Intelligence. He knew everything and let it happen. He didn't bother informing the president - I mean, the Scoundrel - and his quiet was richly rewarded by the new leadership, as you can see. Even with this, because he was unsure of his chances of success, he struck a deal with Abdelghani Abdelghaffar. He would avoid the front lines while communicating with the guys attacking the presidential palace, the Broad-casting House, and other government strong-holds. Mamduh drank at that exclusive Club till the last minute, then proceeded to worship in the Grand Mosque with the members of the Revolutionary Committee. As a result, he was appointed Minister of the Interior. That was no longer a game for him. He would be safe if the coup failed, but as it succeeded, he was cat-apulted to the front stage because it succeeded. What are your thoughts about that?

He grinned airily as if he were telling me a clever joke. He, on the other hand, was not amused. It wasn't precisely what I anticipated to hear from him regarding the new regime's top administration. I'd feel confident if he con-firmed to me Mamdouh was faithful. I may not have agreed with all of his points of view, but it is much easier to deal with a man whose behaviour is harmonious with his beliefs. So how could any guy feel safe with a chameleon?

Such outrageous behaviour shocked me, and I'm unsure if the Emir was an Islamist or an illusionist! I'm not surprised Sophia divorced. I felt respect for her. Mamdouh is not the kind of man any reasonable woman would trust. He is a snake, a weathercock, and an alligator! Such an insult to the Islamic Revolution almost outraged me. A drunk at the helm of the most powerful Ministry? It's extraordinary, unbefitting of Abdelghani Abdelghaffar.

I'm sure his narrowed eyes are for something in this terrible deal. But, unfortunately, Abdelghani missed his aim again: he put the wrong man in the wrong position! Alas!

– Surprised? Look, Mr Bassam, politics might differ from what most people believe. It is not just the art of administering public affairs but also the art of concealing private matters from the public. That's how it works, and you should get used to it because that's our reality. You can work to the top when you understand this and learn to ignore it. I obtained this post because I am wise, not because of my brother-in-law. It was not difficult for me to acquire the Committee of Revolution's trust, as I had spent several years working in close collaboration with military intelligence. During those years, I learnt to close my eyes and my ears to some facts for one simple reason: the truth, the full truth, does not exist anywhere, and even if it existed, it would serve no purpose, for nobody wants to hear it. When I realised that the government was in its last days, I worked to strengthen my connections to the men of the future without fully separating from the other side. As a result, I was awarded a top post. I was lucky. Nevertheless, I worked hard. Mister Bassam, you may be no less blessed. Let's forget about what you did before the Revolution. No one knows about it, and those who do - I'm talking about the ex-Director of Security and some of his men - can no longer hurt you. I will support you. The fact that you were incarcerated under the Scoundrel's rule is an excellent make-believe. As a result, you will serve as one of my men; you will be my eyes and ears. I'll introduce you to Mamdouh as soon as it's possible. For your part, you will sign the project we have discussed, allowing me to notify the Ministry of Finance. There wouldn't be any objections. We need to reorganise the banking sector, and your suggestions would be appreciated.

He stopped before adding, "I'll let you change your clothing. You'd need to shower as well. After that, I'll provide orders for your convenience. It is pointless for you to come with me to the workplace immediately. Take your time; I've already told you everything you need to know. I'll send the car to pick you up at seven this evening. After that, we'll have dinner with Sophia. Is everything all right?

– It's all right, sir, I responded, surprised. Then, after reflecting on what had occurred, I continued thoughtfully: I'd like to make another request. I wish to visit 'Ouja. I'm afraid I'll be late for the funerals but I want to go to the cemetery.

– That's understandable. We'll take care of it as quickly as we can. (He took a breath.) I'll be gracious. Is this dinner so urgent? No. Let's put it off till you return from your village. That will give you time to think clearly and prepare yourself.

– Sir, I am quite thankful to you. I don't know how to express my gratitude for everything you've done for me.

– Never mind! Bassam, you're my brother, and this is my responsibility. First, visit the graves of your bereaved family. They have become our martyrs. Return to the capital after that. I'll reserve a room for you at the Sheraton. Don't be concerned about anything.

The chauffeur will arrive at seven o'clock as arranged. Is there anything else you'd like to enquire about?

I paused.

– In truth, sir, I don't dare to ask you.

– What's the problem? Please inform me right now.

– Ahem... um... I'm curious about what happened to Mr Aroussi. I don't see him any longer. You see, he was my boss for a long time. He hired a lawyer on my behalf. I still respect him since I know he cares about my career.

He looked at me blankly.

– Hey! Bassam, you're a strange man. Your loyalty has greatly impressed me. I hope you continue to be so forthright in the future. Nonetheless, I want to ensure you know your former boss. He was secluded, which is why you don't see him about. I feel bad for him, but as talented and competent as he is, there is so much evidence against him. He used to smuggle foreign currencies out of the country, and the man who worked for him confessed completely before his death. Additionally, un-like you, he was not operating in secret, but everyone is aware of his close ties to the regimes of the Scoundrel and the King. Unfortunately, I'm unable to help him.

I ducked mutely.

– I know a lot about him, he added. He was my chamber mate. Mr Ammar, one of the best solicitors in the country, is his broth-er-in-law. He will defend him brilliantly, far better than I can. So don't be concerned about that guy, Bassam. Sharks like him are always able to escape from any trap. (He hesitated). I don't need to tell you that this conversation never happened. Everything you learnt today will be useful if you keep your mouth shut. If you act wisely, you will rise faster than you ever anticipated or hoped. It is not improbable that you may receive a decoration one day.

It seemed too good to be true! I imagined myself standing in front of Emir Abdelghani Abdelghaffar. The latter was awkwardly attempting to catch the button on my jacket while failing to hang the medal on my chest. He would make the identical action thrice, unsuccessfully and once successfully. After that, I'd be a national hero like Hamda La'war. That's my life's ambition, the crowning career achievement, the fulfilment of my senior age.

At last, I find a government fair enough to recognise the great services I would owe to it; a government ready to pay for the debts of its predecessors by making me a man indebted forever. Oh my God! My dear, my omnipotent, my merciful God! Thank you a thousand times. No, thank you. Two hundred thousand, or better... two hundred million times, that is as much as I have on my credit account. I was still perplexed. I couldn't believe it. I smiled. Grace and beatitude enveloped me. I was going to start dancing and get into a trance. In my nirvana, I would yell, rejoice, leap, and kiss my benefactor's rubicund beard. I would kiss everyone I saw along the path, including Frankenstein, Zorro, and the black guard. Now that everything has been counted, I prefer not to kiss them. My zeal blinded me to the calamity that had befallen my family. The consolation for my biggest loss was so quick, unexpected, beautiful, rewarding, and soothing that it was almost impermissible. I tried to keep myself under control and stop the flood of emotions that washed over me.

I muttered meekly after a long interval of stillness:

– Are you... um... certain, sir? Is it... um... Is this some joke?

Hassan looked at me with suspicious green eyes.

– A joke? What are you talking about, lad?

– Nothing, sir. It's all about... um... the medal. Is it a pledge?

He appeared perplexed by my enquiry.

– A pledge? So, let's suppose it is; sure. But, it is up to you to contribute to its success.

I was pulled in.

– Do you believe the Emir will grant it to me? He has no idea who I am or what I am up to, sir. But I am the Revolution's most humble servant. Nonetheless, I am living a dream. I paid a high price for supporting the Revolution, as I lost both my mother and my fiancée. Sir, I'm still shocked.

– The Emir has no idea who you are, but we'll make him aware of your presence, Mr Bassam.

I'm quite sure he wasn't kidding. So what the hell is going on? But I wanted to be certain.

– Would Sophia be pleased if I am... um... decorated?

I couldn't help but notice his cheerful glance.
- Oh! Yes, very much so. She'd like it if her husband was a national hero.

"Her husband" rang out in my brain "her husband? Is she not divorced?" I asked rashly.

That bothered him:

– Yeah, I'm referring to you, fool. You're going to be the husband.

I was almost taken aback by his self-assurance. He had sealed my destiny without even considering my input. I had yet to meet his sister. All I knew about her was that she had three children. It seems that the agreement between us was mostly founded on this marriage. He had no doubt I would accept marrying his sister even if she was hard of hearing and squinting or blind!! Was she, however, truly so? I was terrified. Yet, that was the condition of my release; that much is certain. What if I refused? The solution was no less straightforward. Like all traitors, I would be beheaded in public! All counts have been completed. I'd rather marry Sophia. I rapidly calculated the stakes. I couldn't sit around any longer. My trials were harsh and useless to him since I knew he'd gone insane with that obsessive obsession.

– Yes, I said. You are correct, sir. Indeed, I am her husband.

– Well, let's hope she agrees now. Try to be kind to her. Refrain from bringing up your tortuous story. Nevertheless, I'll be there for dinner. We'll discuss everything when you return from 'Ouja.

As two excellent friends, we shook hands enthusiastically. He then marched across the room to his foot soldiers in the courtyard. The grey uniforms straightened and saluted as they saw him. The sun was blazing and beaming brightly over the entire world.

It was an unusually misty morning for me, despite the shining sun... The morning of the mogul.

Stay Tuned ... More Coming.